Ready Steady Read!

Dear Parents,

Congratulations! Your child has embarked on an exciting journey – they're learning to read! As a parent, you can be there to support and cheer them along as they take their first steps.

At school, children are taught how to decode words and arrange these building blocks of language into sentences and wonderful stories.

At home, parents play a vital part in reinforcing these new-found skills. You can help your child practise their reading by providing well-written, engaging stories, which you can enjoy together.

This series – **Ready, Steady, Read!** – offers exactly that, and more. These stories support inexperienced readers by:

- gradually introducing new vocabulary
- using repetition to consolidate learning
- gradually increasing sentence length and word count
- providing texts that boost a young reader's confidence.

As each book is completed, engaging activities encourage young readers to look back at the story, while a Picture Dictionary reinforces new vocabulary. Enjoyment is the key – and reading together can be great fun for both parent and child!

Prue Goodw

Lecturer

How to use this series

The **Ready, Steady, Read!** series has 4 levels.
The facing page shows what you can expect to find
in the books at each level.

As your child's confidence grows, they can progress
to books from the higher levels. These will keep them
engaged and encourage new reading skills.

The levels are only meant as guides; together, you and
your child can pick the book that will be just right.

Here are some handy tips for helping children who are
ready for reading!

Give them choice – Letting children pick a book
(from the level that's right for them) makes them
feel involved.

Talk about it – Discussing the story and the
pictures helps children engage with the book.

Read it again – Repetition of favourite stories
reinforces learning.

Cheer them on! – Praise and encouragement
builds a child's confidence and the belief in their
growing ability.

LEVEL 1 For first readers

* short, straightforward sentences
* basic, fun vocabulary
* simple, easy-to-follow stories of up to 100 words
* large print and easy-to-read design

LEVEL 2 For developing readers

* longer sentences
* simple vocabulary, introducing new words
* longer stories of up to 200 words
* bold design, to capture readers' interest

LEVEL 3 For more confident readers

* longer sentences with varied structure
* wider vocabulary
* high-interest stories of up to 300 words
* smaller print for experienced readers

LEVEL 4 For able readers

* longer sentences with complex structure
* rich, exciting vocabulary
* complex stories of up to 400 words
* emphasis on text more than illustrations

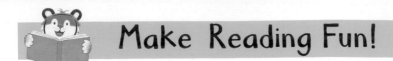
Once you have read the story, you will find some amazing activities at the back of the book! There are Excellent Exercises for you to complete, plus a super Picture Dictionary.

But first it is time for the story . . .

Ready?

Steady?

Let's read!

M Christina Butler   Daniel Howarth

Who's Been Eating My Porridge?

LITTLE TIGER PRESS
London

Little Bear would not eat his porridge. "No porridge!" he said.

"Then I will give it to Scary Bear," said Mummy, taking it outside.

All that day Little Bear watched
out for Scary Bear.

"I don't think there *is* a Scary Bear," he said that evening.

"Well, somebody has eaten your porridge," said Mummy.

The next morning, Daddy put honey on Little Bear's porridge.

"I don't like porridge!" cried Little Bear.

So Daddy Bear left it outside for Scary Bear.

That afternoon, Granny and
Grandpa came to stay.

"I hear you're not eating your
porridge," said Grandpa. "No wonder
there's a Scary Bear about. Scary
Bears love porridge."

Sure enough, Little Bear's bowl
was empty again!

The next day,
Granny put some
berries on Little Bear's
porridge. But Little Bear
still wouldn't eat it.

So Grandpa took
the porridge
outside again.

Little Bear's cousins came to visit
that afternoon.

They played Scary Bear games
amongst the trees.

On the way home, Little Bear
was very quiet.

So Daddy Bear tucked
him into bed.

That night, Little Bear dreamed
that Scary Bear was chasing him.

"I want your porridge," he growled.

"You're not having it!"
Little Bear shouted.

And he sat down
and ate it all up.
Then he woke up.

At breakfast, Little Bear
ate one bowl of porridge . . .

Then he ate another one!

All day he helped put honey into jars.

Suddenly, there was a noise outside.

There, in front of the den, were lots of little animals, all shouting, "Where's our porridge?"

"So that's who Scary Bear is!" giggled Little Bear.

Now every morning, when Little
Bear has eaten his porridge, he takes
another bowl outside for '*Scary Bear*'.
And '*he*' always eats it!

**Have you read the story? Well done!
Now it is time for more fun!**

Here are some questions about the story. Ask an adult to
listen to your answers, and help if you get stuck.

Perfect Porridge

Little Bear learns to love porridge in this story. What do
you like to eat for breakfast?

Happy Helper

Now describe what Little Bear is doing in this picture.
How do *you* like to help out in the kitchen?

Angry Animals

Can you name all the animals in this picture?

Scaredy Bear

Can you remember what happened in Little Bear's dream? What things have *you* dreamed about?

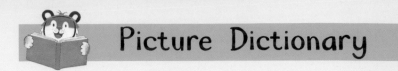 # Picture Dictionary

Can you read all of these words from the story?

bear

bed

berries

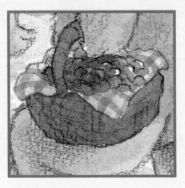

bowl

eat

Grandpa

honey

jars

ran

trees

Can you think of any other words that describe these pictures – for example, what colours can you see? Why not try to spell some of these words? Ask an adult to help!

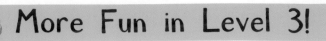

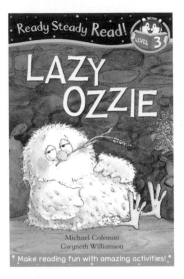

Lazy Ozzie

Lazy Ozzie is too lazy to learn how to fly. So he thinks of a brilliant plan to fool his mum into thinking he can. But will Ozzie's mum be so easily fooled . . . ?

Little Mouse and the Big Red Apple

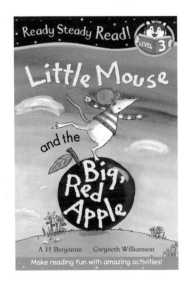

Mouse does not want to share his big, juicy apple but he is too small to move it on his own. Can he get his friends to help and still eat it all himself?

Nobody Laughs at a Lion!

"I'm the King of the Jungle because I'm the best!" says Pa Lion. But each time he shows off his skills, the other animals start to giggle. Don't they know that NOBODY laughs at a lion?

Ridiculous!

One snowy day, Shelley leaves her cosy bed to go on an adventure. But whoever heard of a tortoise out in winter . . . ?
Ridiculous!

Especially for Daniel Cautley and Max Henry with love — M C B
To Mum and Dad, thank you
And to my little bears, who love their porridge — D H

LITTLE TIGER PRESS, 1 The Coda Centre, 189 Munster Road, London SW6 6AW
First published in Great Britain 2004
This edition published 2013
Text copyright © M Christina Butler 2004, 2013
Illustrations copyright © Daniel Howarth 2004, 2013
Printed in China
978-1-84895-677-3
LTP/1800/0597/0413
2 4 6 8 10 9 7 5 3 1

Books in the Series

LEVEL 1 - For first readers

Can't You Sleep, Dotty?

Fred

My Turn!

Rosie's Special Surprise

What Bear Likes Best!

LEVEL 2 - For developing readers

Hopping Mad!

Newton

Ouch!

Where There's a Bear, There's Trouble!

The Wish Cat

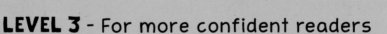

LEVEL 3 - For more confident readers

Lazy Ozzie

Little Mouse and the Big Red Apple

Nobody Laughs at a Lion!

Ridiculous!

Who's Been Eating My Porridge?

LEVEL 4 - For able readers

The Biggest Baddest Wolf

Meggie Moon

Mouse, Mole and the Falling Star

The Nutty Nut Chase

Robot Dog